Finney's Big Break

Doug and Debbie Kingsriter

Illustrated by Ann Iosa

WORD Kids!

WORD PUBLISHING
Dallas·London·Vancouver·Melbourne

Our thanks to:
Laura Minchew for believing that
all of us need to care for God's Earth;
Laura Minchew and Brenda Ward for creating this
book series to encourage little and big people alike
to do what we can to be good stewards of our world;
and all the children who are teaching us, by example,
to take care of God's beautiful earth.

Other Books in the
Save God's Earth Series:

Gilroy's Goof
Clipper's Crazy Race

Finny's Big Break
Copyright © 1992 by Doug and Debbie Kingsriter for the text.
Copyright © 1992 by Ann Iosa for the illustrations.

Library of Congress Cataloging-in-Publication Data

Kingsriter, Debbie, 1951–
   Finny's Big Break/ by Debbie and Doug Kingsriter; illustrated
by Ann Iosa.
      p.   cm. — (Save God's Earth)
   Summary: The pollution in Patton's Pond reaches the disaster stage when Finny, a
fish, is entrapped in a bottle: and it takes the ingenuity of the pond animals and the
kindness of neighboring children to save Finny and clean up the pond.
   ISBN 0-8499-0920-1
   [1. Fishes—Fiction. 2. Pond animals—Fiction. 3. Water—Pollution—Fiction
4. Pollution—Fiction.] I. Kingsriter, Doug. II. Iosa, Ann, ill. III. Title. IV. Series:
Kingsriter, Debbie. 1951– Save God's Earth
PZ7.K618Fi 1992
[E]—dc20   92–12325
                                                                        CIP
                                                                        AC

Printed in the United States of America

2345679 LBM 987654321

To our children,
Lauren, Barrett, and Blake,
but especially Barrett, whose dreams are as wide
as the oceans and filled with as many wonders

It was morning, and the sun's light had come to splash in Patton's Pond. Bright colors burst through the quiet water toward the little fish sleeping below.

Finian Flanagan III felt the sun's warmth and opened one eye. He was still sleepy, but he had to get moving. Finny, as everyone called him, was the Official Waker Upper of Patton's Pond.

Finny opened his other eye. "Time to wake everybody up!" he said with a smile.

Each morning while the other fish yawned and stretched, Finny would race 'round and 'round. Then, with a flick of his tail, he'd turn upward. And he'd break through the surface like an underwater missile.

"It's morning!" he'd yell to his friends Slip the Frog and Slide the Duck. Then Finny would hit the water and flip like a porpoise. That's why everyone loved Finny—he was so much fun! Slip and Slide would giggle with glee. Their laughter made the funniest sounds you could ever imagine. If you were there, you'd laugh, too, even if you were grumpy that day.

Suddenly a loud KERPLUNK! broke the quiet. Finny looked up
and saw something big coming at him. KABLONK! It bounced off
a nearby rock and almost hit him. Finny looked out from around
the rock. The unfriendly thing was standing in the sand on the
bottom of the pond. It was a big bottle.

Finny had never seen one like it before. But he knew that it didn't belong in the water. The little fish was angry. He didn't want trash in his home.

"I'm going to knock that thing down!" said Finny.
Slip and Slide saw bubbles coming up and peeked through the
lily pads. Paddle the Beaver swam down to see what was going
on. Even Snoozing Carp watched what Finny was doing.

Just then, Finny flipped his tail. But instead of knocking the bottle down, something terrible happened.

"Watch out!" Slip yelled to Finny, but it was too late! SQUEEZZUNK! Finny was stuck . . . then unstuck . . . then BAM! he hit his head on something hard.

From inside the bottle, everything looked different. Even Slip the Frog's face looked strange. When Finny tried to swim, he bumped his nose on the glass walls. He tried to turn around so he could wiggle out, but there wasn't enough room. He tried to swim backward, but the bottle was too narrow. He was trapped!

Everyone tried to think of ways to get Finny out. Slip kicked the bottle. Paddle slapped the bottle with his tail. Snapping Turtle tried to bite a hole in the bottle. But nothing worked. Finny was still stuck. His friends couldn't help him.

Poor Finny! No one had ever seen him so sad. If the pond weren't so wet, everyone would have known that Finny was crying.

Slip crawled up on his lily pad to catch his breath. Slide swam in little circles with her head hanging low. They were very un-happy. "We won't ever get to play with Finny again," Slide sadly quacked.

SPLASH! Two children were swimming near the dock. They were on a picnic with their parents.

Slide hurried over to her friend. "I've got an idea!" she quacked excitedly. "Maybe those kids can get Finny out!"

Slip listened to Slide's idea. Then he croaked a happy croak and plopped into the water.

Soon every fish in the pond was jumping out of the water above Finny. "Look over there!" Susan Woods said to her brother, Matt. She pointed to the fish leaping and flopping.

"Hey, let's get a closer look!" Matt yelled. They quickly swam to the spot where the fish were jumping.

Under the water Slip went to work. He made sure that the jumping fish stayed close to the bottle. When the children got closer, he pushed the bottle in front of Matt.

"What's this?" said Matt. And he reached down to pull something from the water.

Little Finny was terrified! His friends waved a tearful good-bye. They sure hoped their plan would work. What would they do without Finny?

"It's just a bottle," said Matt. "We might as well throw it back."
"We can't do that, Matt," said Susan. "The bottle doesn't belong
in the pond. And look! There's a little fish in it!" Both children
stared at poor Finny. "A fish in a bottle?" wondered Matt.

"Let's show it to Mom and Dad!" said Susan. Off she went carrying the bottle with Finny inside.

"Hey, wait for me!" hollered Matt. He stopped to grab their towels.

When Matt got to the picnic area, Susan was already showing the bottle to their Mom and Dad.

"Poor little fish," said Susan. "Wonder how he got in there?"

"Things like that happen when people don't take care of God's creation," said Mrs. Woods.

"Is there any way we can get it out?" asked Matt.

"I think we can find a way to save this little fellow," said Mr. Woods. And he reached for a bucket of water near his tackle box.

"Noah saved the animals in his day," said Susan. "He protected them from the flood. If we can save this little fish, we can help God, too, just like Noah did."

"That's a nice thought," said Mrs. Woods. "God wants us all to take care of His creation."

"If Noah hadn't followed God's instructions, we wouldn't have all the animals we have today," Matt said earnestly.

SPLURT! Just then Mr. Woods got Finny out of the bottle.

The children squealed with delight when they saw their fish swimming in the bucket of water. Finny was free . . . well, almost.

"Good work, Dad," said Susan.

Together the Woods family walked down the path toward the pond.

As they knelt to return Finny to his home, Susan pointed out other bottles and cans in the water.

"Throwing pop bottles in the pond sure isn't taking care of God's creation," said Matt.

"You're right, Matt," said Susan. "I think we should do something about it."

"First let's put this little fish back in the water," said her mother. "Then you can tell us what you're thinking about."

SPLASH! When Finny felt the cool water of Patton's Pond he leaped for joy. Then he did a double flip over the lily pads. He was free! He was home! When Slip and Slide saw Finny, they danced with excitement! The plan had worked! News of Finny's return spread quickly around the pond. He was back, safe and sound.

That afternoon the Woods put Susan's plan to work as excited children noisily approached the pond.

"We can start over here," Susan said as she walked toward the place where they had released Finny. "Now, where's our wading team?"

Mr. Woods, Matt, and several other kids finished putting on flippers, gloves, and snorkels. Then they stepped in knee-deep.

Mrs. Woods stood on the bank of the pond. She used a garden rake to pull the bottles, cans, and plastic cups from the water. Others carefully gathered the trash in recycling bags.

Soon the big job was done. The kids planted "Keep Patton's Pond Clean" signs around the pond and picnic area. And everyone cheered. They were very proud of what they had done.

But the loudest cheer came from Patton's Pond. All the little fish flipped and splashed. Slide the Duck quacked her loudest. Paddle the Beaver clapped the water with her tail. And Slip the Frog croaked loud and long.

They were all happy to have a clean home. But most of all they were glad to have their Official Waker Upper back. Little Finny would always be the Brave Hero of Patton's Pond.

Things You Can Do

- Save water — don't let the water run when you brush your teeth. Keep a water pitcher in the refrigerator for a cold drink instead of letting the water run until it's cool. You can save 20,000 gallons a year by not letting the water run needlessly — enough to fill a large swimming pool!

- Adopt a stream or a beach. Make it a classroom or family project to patrol a specific area to keep it clean. Plan a party where you and your friends plant trees along stream banks. This keeps soil from washing into the stream and protects the animals who live there.

- With scissors, cut each ring on plastic six-pack holders. Birds, fish, and even small animals can get caught in these and die.

- Hold on to helium balloons. They can blow over the ocean, and once they pop they will become dangerous to ocean creatures.